VERONICA THE VULTURE

Veronica was feeling sad.

"Why are you feeling sad, Veronica?" asked a Viking called Vincent the Vast.

"I'm feeling sad because I've lost something starting with the letter 'v'," Veronica explained. Vincent did not know what Veronica was looking for.

Veronica was feeling very sad.

"Why are you feeling sad, Veronica?" asked a vampire playing a violin.

"I'm looking for something that starts with the letter 'v' and is the colour violet," Veronica explained. The vampire did not know what Veronica was looking for.

Veronica was feeling very, very sad.

"Why are you feeling sad, Veronica?" asked some vegetables wearing velvet tuxedos.

"I'm looking for something that starts with the letter 'v', is the colour violet, and makes a loud noise," Veronica explained. The vegetables did not know what Veronica was looking for.

Veronica was feeling very, very, very sad.

"Why are you feeling sad, Veronica?" asked a viper playing volleyball.

"I'm looking for something that starts with the letter 'v', is the colour violet, makes a loud noise and cleans things," Veronica explained. The viper did not know what Veronica was looking for.

Veronica was feeling very, very, very, very sad.

"Why are you feeling sad, Veronica?" asked a volcano going on vacation.

"I'm looking for something that starts with the letter 'v', is the colour violet, makes a loud noise, cleans things and has a long handle," Veronica explained.

The volcano got excited, "Oh, I know what you're looking for! I saw one of those on Venus. I'm going there right now if you would like to come with me!"

So Veronica went to Venus.

"Are you looking for something?" asked a village of vinegar. Veronica explained what she was looking for and told them that her new volcano friend said it could be on Venus. The village of vinegar cheered and cleared the way for Veronica to find...

Her vacuum cleaner! "There it is! My vacuum cleaner! Mum is going to be so happy I can clean my room."

Veronica got home and cleaned her room so she was finally allowed to play video games.

Veronica was feeling very, very, very, very happy!

THE
END

CPSIA information can be obtained at www.ICGtesting.com
Printed in the USA
BVIW120745311220
596745BV00031B/60

9 780645 045420